The Wizard
Who Saved the World

Jeffrey Bennett

Illustrated by
Roberta Collier-Morales

Editing: Joan Marsh
Design and Production: Mark Stuart Ong, Side By Side Studios

Published in the United States by
Big Kid Science
Boulder, Colorado 80304
www.BigKidScience.com

ISBN: 978-0-9721819-4-5

Also available in Spanish

Also by Jeffrey Bennett

For children:
Max Goes to the Moon
Max Goes to Mars
Max Goes to Jupiter
Max Goes to the Space Station
I, Humanity

For grownups:
A Global Warming Primer
What is Relativity?
On Teaching Science
Math for Life
Beyond UFOs

Textbooks:
The Cosmic Perspective series
Life in the Universe
Using and Understanding Mathematics
Statistical Reasoning for Everyday Life

Expert Reviewers
Special thanks to the following individuals who reviewed drafts of this book:

Dr. Pranoti Asher, geologist
Dr. Mary Bigelow, educational consultant
Tyson Brown, National Science Teachers Association
Nicole Lederer, Co-founder, Environmental Entrepreneurs
Mark Levy, educational consultant
Dr. Cherilynn Morrow, Georgia State University
Dr. Nicholas Schneider, University of Colorado
Dr. Will Toor, physicist and Boulder County Commissioner
Dr. Mary Urquhart, University of Texas at Dallas
Dr. Robert S. Webb, National Oceanic and Atmospheric Administration
Helen Zentner, educational consultant

About the Characters

Diego is named for the city of San Diego, where the author spent much of his childhood.

Flora is based on the author's "Grandma Flo" (Flora), who immigrated to the United States from Russia in the first decade of the 20th century. Her 101 years of life allowed her to see humanity at both its best and worst, giving her a perspective that the author has tried to honor with the character in this book.

This book is dedicated to all the young wizards who will help save the world, and especially to my own two wizards, Grant and Brooke.

Cara—
Be a Wizard!
4/16/19

iego loved to daydream. During soccer practice, he became a sports hero, scoring the winning goal in the World Cup. When he listened to music, he saw himself performing in front of a sold-out arena. At school, he was a great scientist, shaking hands with the King of Sweden as he received the Nobel Prize. Before bed, he'd look up at the stars, and imagine himself as an astronaut exploring new worlds.

Most of all, Diego dreamed of being a great wizard with magical powers. If his mom got sick, he'd use his wizardry to cure her. When he saw a kid bullying a friend, he magically silenced the bully, and made the bully feel what his friend felt. When his uncle became a firefighter, he put a magic invisible bubble around him, so he couldn't be hurt. But his latest daydream was about a much bigger job. He wished more than ever before to be a real wizard, because someone needed to save the world.

Diego hadn't always thought about the whole world. When he was younger, he didn't think about much beyond his family, friends, and neighborhood. As he got older, he began to realize that he was part of a much bigger world.

Still, big as our world may seem, in school he learned that it looks tiny and fragile when seen against the blackness of space. Our entire planet Earth is smaller than a sunspot on the Sun, and small enough to be swallowed up in a storm on Jupiter. Earth is so small that if Diego became a giant wizard and held the Sun and planets in his hands, he'd need to take great care not to lose it.

Visualizing Earth

The painting shows our wizard with the Sun and planets at their correctly scaled sizes. As you can see, Earth is indeed much smaller than a sunspot, and smaller than the storm on Jupiter known as the Great Red Spot.

The painting does *not* show the orbits of the planets on the same scale. The reason is that planets are really tiny compared to their orbits. To show the planet orbits on the same scale as the planet sizes, we'd need to make the orbits more than a thousand times as big as they are in the painting.

You can get a better sense of what space really looks like by visiting a scale model of the solar system, such as the *Voyage* model in Washington, DC (photo below). There, the Sun is the size of a large grapefruit, while Earth is smaller than the ballpoint in a pen and is 15 meters (49 feet) from the model Sun. As Diego learned, Earth really does look tiny and fragile in the vastness of space.

The *Voyage* model. The gold ball on the nearest pedestal is the Sun, and the other pedestals hold the planets. To learn more about *Voyage*, visit www.voyagesolarsystem.org.

EARTH

Sometimes he'd laugh when he thought of being a giant wizard. He'd picture our world accidentally slipping from his hand, and then searching frantically for the lost Earth. It was, after all, like a tiny jewel. For Diego knew that, in all the vastness of space, we have yet to discover another world on which we could survive outdoors without a spacesuit, even for a few minutes.

Jewel of Life

You've probably read stories and seen movies in which other worlds have people or aliens walking around. But if such worlds exist at all, they must be few and far between. As Diego recognizes, we do not yet know of even a single other world with air that we could breathe, or with life of any kind.

In our solar system, we have sent space-craft to photograph and study all of the planets and their major moons, so we know a lot about them. While it's possible that a few worlds could have some type of life (an idea you can read about in the books *Max Goes to Mars* and *Max Goes to Jupiter*), no other world in our solar system has surface oceans of water or oxygen that we could breathe.

We know much less about planets in other solar systems, by which we mean planets that orbit stars besides our Sun. Stars are so far away that we have only recently been able to discover planets around them, and our telescopes are not yet powerful enough to take pictures that would tell us whether any of these planets have life, oceans, or breathable air.

As a result, there is still great debate among scientists about whether planets like Earth are rare or common around other stars. Nevertheless, given the great distances between stars, there is no doubt that finding a planet like Earth is far more difficult than finding the rarest of jewels. That is why we say that Earth is a jewel of life in the universe.

Diego also remembered learning that we live not only in a special place, but in a special time.

Earth has been around for a long time, but it has not always been like it is today. For most of Earth's history, the air had so little oxygen that we could not have breathed. There have also been ice ages, in which many of our cities would have been buried deeply under ice, and other time periods in which it was so warm that there were no ice caps at all.

Our Place in Time

Scientific study shows that we do indeed live in a special time on Earth.

By studying the oldest rocks that we can find (which are actually meteorites that have fallen to Earth from space), scientists have learned that Earth was born about 4½ billion years ago. Some fossils of microscopic life are almost 4 billion years old, so we know that there has been life on Earth for a very long time. But rocks and fossils also show that there was no oxygen early in Earth's history, and enough oxygen for us to breathe only during the past few hundred million years. It's a remarkable fact: If you had a time machine and spun the dial to visit a random point in Earth's history, you'd have only about a 1 in 10 chance of being able to breathe when you walked out.

Careful study of rocks and fossils also helps us learn about the past climate. Scientists have discovered that the climate has gone through numerous ice ages, during which many of our present-day cities would have been buried under thick ice. Between the ice ages, there have been much warmer periods, in which polar ice melted and sea level rose enough to flood many regions where people now live.

This scientific study teaches us an important lesson. We live at a time when the climate is well-suited to our large civilization, but we now know that Earth's climate can go through rapid and dramatic changes. If we are not careful, we may cause changes to the climate that could make our lives much more difficult.

But what really makes our time special is the way that we are able to live. Diego had a great-grandmother, Flora, who was very old. He loved hearing her stories about growing up without televisions, telephones, computers, or even supermarkets. Flora had lost childhood friends to diseases that vaccines could now prevent, or that medicines could now easily cure. Not long before Flora was born, there hadn't even been cars, or airplanes.

Diego often wondered how all these amazing things could have come to exist without real wizards. "If our ancestors could somehow visit us," he thought, "they would think that we live magical lives."

Our Magical Lives

Imagine having a time machine, and using it to bring someone who lived a few centuries ago to our world today. Many things that we take for granted would surely seem like magic.

Consider transportation and communication. Just a couple hundred years ago, a trip that we can now drive in a few hours would have taken days by horse, and a trip that we can now make easily by airplane might have taken months, if it were possible at all. The idea of talking to people across the globe by cell phone or computer would have seemed far more magical than pulling a rabbit out of a hat.

Modern medicine is just as amazing. For most of human history, less than half of all children survived to adulthood; today, nearly all do, thanks to vaccines, improved public hygiene, and advanced medical treatments. A century ago, even in the most developed nations, the average adult lived only to about age 50. Today, the average is age 80. If life spans continue to increase at the same rate, then *you* may live to be well over 100.

How have we come to live such seemingly magical lives? As you've probably guessed, the answer has nothing to do with magic, and everything to do with science. Through science, we are able to understand problems so that we can solve them. Each new technology builds upon older ones, so that, over time, what once seemed impossible can become routine. As the famous science fiction writer Arthur C. Clarke once said, "Any sufficiently advanced technology is indistinguishable from magic."

11

Fossil Fuels

You've probably heard a lot about air and water pollution, and know that much of it comes from the way we drill for oil and dig for coal, then burn them to make power. But did you ever wonder why these fuels come out of the ground?

The answer is that oil and coal (along with natural gas) are fossil fuels, so-named because they are made from the remains of life (fossils) that lived and died long ago. Although cartoons often show fossil fuels as the remains of dinosaurs, most fossil fuels come from plants and microscopic life, not from large animals.

Fossil fuels are very important to our civilization today. We get more than three-quarters of our energy from fossil fuels, using them to provide electricity and heat, and to make gasoline and jet fuel.

Unfortunately, fossil fuels also cause problems. For one thing, there's all the pollution, along with disasters like oil spills. For another thing, we're starting to run low on oil, and while there's still a lot of coal, it's difficult to dig it out without danger to coal workers and damage to the environment.

Worst of all, fossil fuels are made mostly of carbon, so that when we use them, they release carbon dioxide into the atmosphere. It is this carbon dioxide that is causing the biggest problem that Diego seeks to solve in this book.

Of course, Diego also knew that not everyone in the world lived the same way. Some of his own relatives lived in places where there wasn't always enough food to eat, or enough doctors to prevent and treat diseases. He knew about waters polluted by oil spills, and air polluted by burning coal, and people killed by terrible wars.

In his daydream, the wizard Diego waved his magical wand to grow food, to vaccinate all the children, to clean the water and air, and to end all the wars.

He told his great-grandmother Flora about his daydreams, and she was proud of his imagination. But she also reminded him that he was forgetting the most important thing.

"Education is the only way that people can make their own futures better," Flora told him.

With a wave of his wand, Diego made schools emerge from nothing, with great teachers, lots of books, and computers.

Global Education

If you're reading this book, you probably go to a good school, with dedicated teachers who can help you learn the things it takes to be successful in the modern world. Not everyone is so lucky.

Around the world, only about half of all children have the opportunity to finish high school, and far fewer get to attend college. There are some places where children never even get a chance to finish elementary school. Sadly, the problem is worse for girls than for boys; almost one in five girls in the world has never been taught to read.

Given that education is the key to better lives, you can see why Diego imagines using magic to build great schools. But no magic is required. Many people are already working to build schools and improve education, even in the poorest countries. You can help by looking up nonprofit organizations that focus on global education. Once you find one you like, you can raise money for it, or donate books and supplies. You might even find one that provides opportunities for you to go in person to a place where you can help.

And while you're working to help others, don't forget your own education. The more you learn, the more you will be able to accomplish when you grow up. Pay particular attention to math and science, which become more and more important as our technology advances. Always remember that the only way to learn is by studying, so be sure to make the effort that you need to succeed.

But one problem was more on Diego's mind than all the others. He'd learned about it in school, and it was the problem that most made Diego believe that we need a wizard to save the world. He decided to tell Flora about it.

"Scientists call it *global warming*, and my teacher demonstrated how it happens by wrapping a blanket around me," said Diego. "A blanket doesn't make any heat, but it warms you up because it traps your own body heat. Our classroom was already warm, and I got so hot that I started to sweat."

Flora nodded quietly, while Diego opened to a picture in a book.

"Earth doesn't wear a blanket, of course," explained Diego, "but a gas in our air called *carbon dioxide* acts a lot like one. This picture shows how it works. We've been adding carbon dioxide to the atmosphere, mostly by using gasoline for our cars and coal for our power plants. The extra carbon dioxide is trapping more heat and making Earth warmer."

"I've noticed the changes in my long life," replied Flora. "Spring comes earlier and fall comes later than it used to, and we seem to have more hot days than I remember from when I was young."

Carbon Dioxide and the Greenhouse Effect

reflected sunlight

infrared light from ground

Weather and Climate

Flora has noticed changes in the weather during her life, but she is only one person living in one place. How can we tell if the whole world is experiencing global warming?

To answer this question, you need to understand the difference between *weather* and *climate*. Weather means things like wind, rain, or temperature that we notice from day to day. Some days the weather is cold and rainy, other days it is warm and sunny. Climate refers to the *average* of the weather over many years. We say that Miami has a warmer climate than New York, even though there may be some days when New York is hotter than Miami.

Global warming means a change in the climate for the entire world. Because we're talking about *climate,* we can notice a change only by finding a pattern that continues for many years or decades; by itself, a single warm or cold year doesn't tell us much. Scientists use a variety of techniques to look for changes in the climate. For the past few decades, measurements made with orbiting spacecraft have allowed scientists to monitor the average temperature of the whole world. For the century before that, scientists can figure out what the climate was like by referring to temperature records from weather stations around the world. Going back further, scientists can learn about climate through careful study of things such as tree rings, "ice cores" drilled out of ancient glaciers, sea floor sediments, and fossils.

That is how we have learned that Earth has been through many ice ages and warm periods in the past. It is also how we have learned that, as Flora noticed, the world's overall climate really has been getting warmer during her long lifetime.

15

Too Much of a Good Thing

Diego is right: Without carbon dioxide, Earth would be too cold for liquid water or life. Amazingly, carbon dioxide keeps our planet livable despite being a very small part of Earth's atmosphere. The carbon dioxide concentration recently surpassed 400 parts per million (or "ppm" for short), which means there are about 400 carbon dioxide molecules among every 1 million molecules of air.

Now consider Venus. Although Venus is closer to the Sun than Earth, calculations show that it would also be frozen if it didn't have any carbon dioxide. But in reality, Venus's surface is a sizzling 880°F (470°C), which makes it far hotter than a pizza oven. What makes Venus so incredibly hot? It has a thick atmosphere made almost entirely of carbon dioxide. In total, Venus has about 170,000 times as much atmospheric carbon dioxide as Earth.

We are not in any danger of making our planet as hot as Venus, but the lesson should still be clear. Venus provides absolute proof that carbon dioxide can make a world far hotter than it would be otherwise. So while the carbon dioxide that exists naturally in Earth's atmosphere is a good thing for life, we should be very careful about adding more. As the story says, it's possible to have too much of a good thing.

"Do you know what's really amazing?" asked Diego. "If there was no carbon dioxide at all, Earth would be so cold that the whole planet would be frozen, and nothing could live here. So it's a good thing that we have some carbon dioxide in our atmosphere."

"But that doesn't mean that more is better," he continued. "The planet Venus has so much carbon dioxide that its surface is hotter than a pizza oven! My teacher likes to say that if carbon dioxide is a good thing for life on Earth, Venus is proof that it's possible to have too much of a good thing."

Flora laughed, but then she asked a serious question. "You're teaching me a lot, my Diego. But how do you know that we're really putting more carbon dioxide into the air?"

"I asked my teacher the same thing," he replied. "It turns out that scientists can measure it. A poster in our classroom shows the measurements, and the amount of carbon dioxide just keeps going up. The measurements also tell us that the extra carbon dioxide is coming from our use of gasoline and coal."

"I'm glad to see you paying such close attention in school," said Flora.

Evidence of Global Warming

Diego says that global warming is a serious problem, which is why he wants to become the wizard who saves the world. But you've probably heard that some people doubt that it's a real problem at all. How can you decide who to believe? As with anything in science, the answer is to look at the evidence. In the case of global warming, the scientific evidence is overwhelming — and as easy to understand as 1-2-3. Let's see how.

1. As Diego explained, there's no doubt that carbon dioxide causes a greenhouse effect that traps heat.
2. There's no doubt that we're adding carbon dioxide to the air, because scientists can measure the rising concentration and the added carbon is of a type that only comes from burning fossil fuels.
3. We expect the added carbon dioxide to make Earth warmer, and measurements show that this is indeed happening.

The more carbon dioxide we add, the worse the problem of global warming will become. You can see what's happening in the graphs of carbon dioxide on the classroom wall. The graph for the past few decades shows measurements made directly in our air; the longer graph shows measurements from ice cores drilled in Greenland and Antarctica.

Notice that the amount of carbon dioxide is already higher than it has been for hundreds of thousands of years, and it is rising rapidly — which is why global warming is one of the most serious problems of our time.

Consequences of Global Warming

If global warming only meant a small rise in Earth's average temperature, it might not be so bad. But it has many other consequences. As the story explains, global warming causes what scientists often call *climate change,* meaning changes to local climates.

Some places will warm much more than average, others less. Some places will get more rainfall, which can cause more flooding. Other places will become drier, which can ruin good farmland and lead to more wildfires. We can also expect more extinctions of plants and animals, and great damage to forests and other important ecosystems, because local climates are likely to change faster than many species can adapt.

Changes in climate are not the only expected consequences. Global warming means more heat energy in the atmosphere and more evaporation from the oceans. Heat and evaporation drive winds and storms. That is why global warming can mean more powerful winter blizzards, as well as more severe thunderstorms, more tornados, and more devastating hurricanes.

More carbon dioxide in the air also means that more carbon dioxide will end up dissolved in the oceans, where it makes the ocean water more acidic. This *ocean acidification* is already killing many coral reefs, and some scientists worry that the oceans will no longer be able to produce the seafood that millions of people depend on for survival.

Diego went back to his room, sat down on his bed, and began to daydream about how to save the world. He knew that global warming means a lot more than warmer temperatures. Ice may begin to melt at the polar caps, raising sea level. Storms such as hurricanes and winter blizzards will become more powerful. Some places will get more rainfall, which can cause floods, while other places will become drier and have more wildfires. Global warming even affects the oceans, killing coral reefs and ocean wildlife.

To save the world, Diego imagined becoming a wizard who controlled the climate with a crystal ball. It would take powerful magic, but it might just work.

Suddenly, his mom called him for dinner. Diego snapped out of the daydream. The crystal ball disappeared. His wand and his hat were gone, as were all his magical medicines, and foods, and schools. All that remained were the very real problems of the world. It was depressing.

"We surely need a wizard to save the world," he thought, "but what can I do? I'm only a boy, and I don't suppose I can really grow up to be a wizard."

Rising Sea Level

Global warming will also affect sea level, for two reasons. First, global warming makes the oceans warmer. Just as a balloon expands when you heat it, the oceans will expand as they warm up. Although water expands only a little, there's so much water in the oceans that this effect may cause sea level to rise by 30 centimeters (1 foot) or more during this century, which would mean more coastal flooding during storms.

Second, warmer temperatures can melt ice, and any ice that melts on land, such as the ice in Greenland and Antarctica, will flow into the oceans and raise sea level. (Floating ice, like that in the Arctic Ocean, does not affect sea level when it melts.) There is a lot of landlocked ice on Earth — so much that, if it all melted, sea level would rise more than 70 meters (230 feet)! Fortunately, ice melting is a slow process, so even in the worst case it would probably take many centuries for all the ice to melt. But some melting is probably already under-way, and even a relatively small amount of melting could raise sea level enough to flood many of the world's major coastal cities, and to destroy vast areas of farmland.

No matter how you look at it, global warming is a problem with real consequences. We will have to live with some of these consequences, but surely it would be better to prevent as many of them as possible — and that is something we can do only by finding a way to stop adding so much carbon dioxide to our atmosphere.

Diego talked to his parents and his teacher. They told him to do the best he could, as a real boy and a real person. He talked to Flora, and she gave him more mysterious advice. "There's no such thing as magic," she said, "but you can still be a wizard if you work hard enough." He wasn't sure what she meant, but it got him thinking.

He would start at home, making sure the lights were off when he didn't need them, and replacing old light bulbs with newer, more efficient ones. He'd help his family recycle, and help them drive less. They were small things, but they were a start.

Save a Little, Save a Lot

Small things tend to seem, well, small, but if millions of people do them, they can add up to something big.

Consider light bulbs, for example. Ordinary ("incandescent") light bulbs actually waste most of the energy that they use, because they make a lot of heat in addition to light. That's why they are very hot to the touch. Today, you can buy light bulbs (such as "CFLs" or "LEDs") that make very little heat. As a result, they require only about one-quarter as much energy to make the same amount of light. If everyone replaced their old light bulbs with newer, more efficient ones, we'd need a lot less electricity, and therefore would burn a lot less coal and oil. This wouldn't solve the problem of global warming by itself, but it sure would help.

There are many other small ways in which you can use less energy, and saving energy means using less fuel that puts carbon dioxide into the air. Diego offers a few ideas, but you can probably think of others. Better yet, work with your parents, friends, and teachers to come up with a list of things you can do to save energy. If everyone does it, our reduced need for energy will make it much easier to solve the problem of global warming.

Then he started to think about his future, and what he could do as he grew up. Diego knew that the whole world would have to work together to solve a problem as big as global warming. He also knew that people are best at solving problems when they are healthy and happy.

He didn't have to be a wizard to help with that. He could become a doctor or nurse and help fight off disease, or invent new cures. Or he could work in agriculture to help people grow food with less energy, less waste, and less pollution.

International Action

Global warming is a global problem, because carbon dioxide affects the whole planet, no matter where it comes from. Therefore, even if some countries stopped adding carbon dioxide to the atmosphere, we could still have a problem due to the emissions from other countries.

Can the world really come together to solve a global problem like this? It's happened before. In the 1980s, scientists found out that a different type of gas, called CFCs, was destroying something called *ozone* in Earth's upper atmosphere. This was a major problem, because ozone protects us from dangerous radiation from the Sun. In 1989, countries around the world signed a treaty, usually known as the "Montreal Protocol," that committed everyone to working together to stop the release of ozone-destroying CFCs. The treaty worked, and that is why we no longer worry so much about ozone depletion.

Similar global efforts to slow or stop global warming have been tried several times. These efforts have not yet succeeded, but the ozone treaty shows us that success is possible. Perhaps we all simply need to remember an old saying: "If at first you don't succeed, try, try again."

21

Geoengineering

Because global warming affects the entire Earth, some people have suggested "geoengineering" our planet to fight global warming. For example, some people propose putting millions of tons of small particles into the upper atmosphere, where they would reflect sunlight and thereby cool the planet. Some have even proposed putting giant sunshades in space to accomplish the same thing.

Unfortunately, most geoengineering schemes have a fatal flaw: They don't actually reduce the amount of carbon dioxide in the atmosphere. This leads to two major problems. First, if the schemes ever fail for any reason, such as because people a few centuries from now neglect to maintain the geoengineering projects, then global warming would return almost immediately, and likely much worse than before. Second, while these schemes might reduce warming, they do nothing to reduce the problem of ocean acidification, which could have equally dire consequences.

A few geoengineering ideas might avoid these flaws, perhaps by finding ways to remove carbon dioxide from the atmosphere. Of course, we'd have to be careful not to remove too much, and there could be other unforeseen consequences to deliberately altering our planet. That is why any type of geoengineering should probably be considered only as a last resort.

Maybe he'd work for an important business, or start a business of his own. After all, Flora had once told him that "business is the most powerful force for change in the world."

Or he could go into public service, helping people work together to solve our problems. He could even run for office himself, becoming a legislator, or a Congressman, or the President!

Diego remembered something his teacher had said, about how you really have to understand a problem before you can solve it. Perhaps he should become a scientist, helping us learn more about how the climate works. Or he could study mathematics, or computer programming, since scientists use computers to do the calculations needed to predict how global warming may affect us.

$$T_{no\ greenhouse} = 280°C \sqrt[4]{\frac{(1-reflectivity)}{d^2(AU)}} - 273°C$$

$$Earth: \quad = 280°C \times \sqrt[4]{\frac{(1-0.29)}{1^2}} - 273° = -16°C$$

$$Earth\ actual = 15°C$$

$$\Rightarrow greenhouse$$
$$warming = 31°C$$

Climate on a Computer

Suppose you wanted to know how warmer temperatures would affect the growth of a particular type of plant. You'd probably set up an experiment, in which you'd grow several of these plants, each kept at a different temperature. Now, suppose you want to know how warmer temperatures will affect our entire planet. It would be nice if we could set up a similar experiment, in which we took several Earths and warmed each a different amount. But we can't do that, because we have only one Earth. That's why scientists instead do experiments using *computer models* of Earth.

The basic idea is simple. Just as you can use a computer to simulate driving a car or flying an airplane, scientists can use computers to simulate the way Earth's climate works. The hard part is in the details, because Earth's climate is very complex. Working together, scientists, mathematicians, and computer programmers try to represent the climate with numbers and equations in a computer, and then use the computer to calculate how the climate changes with time.

If these computer models were perfect, then we could understand exactly how global warming will affect us. But there are still many aspects of the climate that scientists don't fully understand. Nevertheless, we can test whether the models are on the right track by seeing if they can successfully "predict" changes to the climate that have already happened. Today's models do this quite well, though not perfectly. That is why, even though we know that global warming is a real problem, we cannot predict all of its precise consequences.

23

Diego was having fun, thinking about all the possibilities that might await him. He could become an engineer, designing electric cars or high-speed trains. He could power them with renewable energy sources, like solar energy and wind power.

Renewable Energy

You've probably heard a lot about *renewable energy* sources, such as energy from sunlight, wind, or tides. These energy sources are getting a lot of attention for three major reasons.

First, as the name tells us, we don't have to worry about running out of renewable energy. After all, the Sun will keep shining, the wind will keep blowing, and tides will keep rising and falling, even if we use them for energy in the meantime. Second, a *lot* of renewable energy is available. For example, the total amount of sunlight reaching Earth each day is more than 5,000 times the amount of energy that our civilization uses each day, and the total energy carried by wind is more than 10 times what we use. Third, and most important to the problem of global warming, renewable energy does not release any carbon dioxide into the atmosphere.

Given these benefits, you might wonder why we don't simply replace all the energy we now get from fossil fuels with renewable energy sources. The answer is that it's not so easy to do, though many people are trying. You may already have solar panels on your home or school, and wind farms are being built in many places. As Diego imagines, perhaps *you* might someday help us figure out better ways to make use of renewable energy, and thereby solve the problem of global warming.

24

He thought of even more amazing ideas. He could study fusion, the power source of the Sun and other stars, and figure out how we could use it to make energy here on Earth. He could find a way to make clean fuels from plants or algae or bacteria. Maybe he could even come up with a way to remove some of the carbon dioxide that we've already released into the atmosphere.

It made him daydream again, imagining the Nobel Prize he'd win for solving the world's energy problems and global warming at the same time.

Fusion

As Diego says, something called *fusion* really is the power source of the Sun and other stars. Here's how it works.

The Sun is made mostly of a gas called *hydrogen*. Deep inside the Sun, the temperature is so hot that tiny particles of hydrogen crash into each other hard enough to stick together, or *fuse*. When the cycle of fusion is complete, the hydrogen has been turned into another gas, called *helium*. This process releases a lot of energy, and this energy is what makes the Sun shine.

There's lots of hydrogen on Earth, too. The H in H_2O, or water, stands for hydrogen. Therefore, if we knew how, we could take hydrogen from water and use it to make energy through fusion. The main byproduct would be safe and useful helium, and no carbon dioxide would be released at all.

Unfortunately, we do not yet know how to build fusion power plants. But imagine that we could, and that you were willing to let us borrow your kitchen sink. If we turned on the faucet, we could extract hydrogen from the water flowing out. If we then fused this hydrogen in our power plant, we could make energy. How much energy? Well . . .

In principle, the water flowing through your kitchen faucet could produce enough fusion energy to replace *all* other energy sources currently used by the entire United States. If four of your friends also lent their faucets, we could generate enough energy for the entire world! Perhaps now you understand why Diego thinks it might be worthwhile to study fusion, in hopes that we will someday be able to build fusion power plants.

Solar Energy from Space

Solar energy has great promise, but on Earth it also has at least a couple of problems. For example, getting all of our energy from sunlight would require covering large areas with solar collectors, which means doing at least some damage to the environment in the process. Also, solar energy works only when it's daytime and sunny, so we'd have to find a way to store energy for nighttime and cloudy days. But as Diego notes, there's a way to get around these problems: Put the solar panels in space.

In space, there are no clouds, and if you put the panels high enough above Earth, they'd be in sunlight at virtually all times. The collected energy could be beamed to ground stations in the form of microwaves. There'd be no carbon dioxide emissions, or any other pollution of any kind. About the only problem would come from the microwave beams, which you wouldn't want to fly through. But these would be easy for aircraft to avoid, and we could locate them away from the migratory routes of birds.

Moreover, unlike the case for fusion, we probably already have the technology needed for solar energy from space. So why don't we do it? The main reason is cost, especially the cost of launching all the solar panels into orbit. Many people are working to bring down the cost of getting into space. If they are successful, solar energy from space could turn out to be a great solution to both our energy problems and global warming.

He could become a teacher, helping people learn the importance of saving our world. He could be an astronomer, discovering more about our place in the amazing universe that surrounds us.

He could even be an astronaut, assembling giant solar panels in space to send energy to Earth, and making trips that would inspire other children to make their own contributions to our future.

The ideas seemed endless. There were so many choices, so many ways that he could help save the world. Diego knew that he only had to work hard and hold on to his dreams to make any of them happen.

Careers and College

As Diego says, there are many careers through which you can help save the world. But there's one thing that most of these careers have in common: They require that you go to college and get a good education.

College may still seem far in your future, but if you hope to go, now is a good time to start building the habits that will make it possible. There's no magic formula, but here are a few suggestions that will help.

Believe in yourself. Even if no one in your family has ever been to college, there's nothing stopping you from being the first. If anyone tells you that you're not smart enough or good enough, prove them wrong.

Read, a lot. The more you read now, the better you'll be prepared for the reading you'll need to do in the future.

Make every subject your favorite. All the subjects you learn in school are important, and they can all be fun, too, if you give them your best effort.

Study every day. Just as more practice will make you better in sports or music, more studying will make you better in school. Do all your homework, and then try to study a little extra. It's especially good to spend extra time on math, which will open the door to many great careers when you grow up.

Accept advice. Parents, teachers, and other grownups around you may not be perfect, but they are usually trying to help you. Listen to what they have to say, and if it makes sense, try to take it to heart.

Most important, hold onto your dreams. As you get older, you may be tempted to think it's too hard to save the world, or that you can't become what you once thought. You can. As Walt Disney famously said, "If you can dream it, you can do it."

Diego felt much better. He had figured out how to save the world, and he didn't even need any magic. He was so excited, he ran to tell his parents and Flora. He ran right past a mirror . . .

. . . and caught a quick glimpse of his reflection. Perhaps it was just his imagination, but it sure looked like he'd become a wizard after all.

Suggested Activities

What Can *You* Do About Global Warming? (Grades 1–8)

Look again at the "small things" that Diego suggests doing on Page 20. Working in small groups, do the following:

- Make a list of small things that you can do on your own, with your family, with your school, or with your community.
- For each item on your list, discuss how you can make sure that you follow through with your planned action.
- Come up with a process for tracking your progress. For example, you might create a log book or a poster on which you can make daily or weekly notations about whether you are succeeding for each item on your list.

How Might Global Warming Affect You? (Grades 4–8)

As we learn from Diego on Page 18, global warming is expected to affect different places in different ways. Learn more about how global warming may affect your community, and what your community can do to adjust. Here are a few ways you might proceed:

- Search the Web for information about local effects; for example, you could search on "local effects of global warming" and then look for information about your area.
- Contact local experts on global warming or climate change, and interview them about what you can expect in your area.
- Once you know what kinds of effects are expected, discuss ways that your community could try to adapt to these effects.

Dream Careers (Grades 4–8)

Pick three different careers that you think would be fun, interesting, and that would let you make a positive impact on the world. For each one:

- Briefly describe what your job would be, and how your job could contribute to making the world a better place.
- Find out what kind of education is needed to get the job.
- Make a brief list of things you can be doing today that might help you achieve the dream of getting this career.